My Best Friend Is Belle

By Lisa Ann Marsoli
Illustrated by the Disney Storybook Artists

Random House 🏠 New York

Library of Congress Control Number: 2005928295

ISBN: 0-7364-2390-7

www.randomhouse.com/kids/disney

MANUFACTURED IN CHINA   10 9 8 7 6 5 4 3 2 1

Ding-a-ling! The bells on the door of the Jolie Bakery jingled. Claire, the baker's daughter, looked up from behind the counter.

"*Bonjour,* Belle!" Claire sang out. "I was hoping you might come in today." Belle often stopped by and read to Claire after a visit to the town library.

"Mmmmm," Belle said, "and just in time for some fresh chocolate croissants, I see!"

Claire noticed Belle's stack of books.

"Are those new?" she asked.

"Actually, these are the ones we read last week," Belle told her. "Shall I make up a story instead?"

"Yes, please!" Claire replied.

While Claire iced a cake, Belle made up a fairy tale about a flying purple dragon that freed an entire kingdom from an evil witch.

"I wish I could make up stories like that," Claire said.

"Have you ever tried?" Belle asked.

"Sometimes I can think of a beginning to a story, but not an end," Claire admitted. "And sometimes I can come up with an end but not a beginning. I don't have a very good imagination."

Claire's father overheard them. "Perhaps you can imagine delivering the bread to our customers," the baker said with a smile.

Belle offered to help Claire make her
deliveries. On their way, they passed the
dressmaker's shop. In the window was a dress as
fancy as a wedding cake.

"Madame Cosette designs all the gowns
herself," Claire remarked. "She's so talented!"

"Indeed she is," agreed Belle.

As they passed the florist's shop, Claire said, "Madame Fleuret is so good at putting the right flowers and colors in her bouquets."

Belle noticed that Claire seemed troubled. She asked the little girl what was the matter.

"Everyone in our village is good at something—except for me," Claire said.

"You can make up wonderful stories, the dressmaker can design beautiful dresses, and Madame Fleuret can take a bunch of ordinary flowers and turn them into a work of art," Claire told Belle. "I want to make something beautiful and creative, too."

"Everyone has something special they can do," replied Belle. "You just need to discover what that something is."

From that moment on, Claire was determined to find her own special skill.

The very next day, when Belle walked into the bakery, Claire rushed out from behind the counter with a big box.

"For you!" Claire said proudly. "I designed it all by myself."

"Why, thank you!" Belle replied, surprised. She untied the ribbon, lifted the lid, and pulled out a dress. It was sewn from patches of mismatched fabric. One sleeve was attached near the waist, and the buttons were all out of place.

Belle didn't know what to say. Luckily, Claire said it for her.

"Goodness, it's ugly—isn't it?" The little girl started to giggle.

Belle smiled. "Well, it is unusual," she admitted.

"Bad news," Claire announced to Belle a few days later. "I tried writing poetry, but I'm terrible." She read it aloud. . . .

"Sometimes when I roll out the dough,
The rolling pin drops on my toe.
While in the oven the tart bakes,
Alas, my foot still throbs and aches!"

"You're good at writing a funny poem," Belle pointed out.

"That's the problem," Claire replied. "I wasn't trying to be funny."

The following afternoon, Claire decided to visit Belle at the cottage she shared with her father, Maurice.

"I want you to be completely honest," Claire told Belle as she unrolled a portrait she had just painted.

"It's . . . um . . . very interesting," Belle said gently. "Is it Madame Fleuret's dog, Gigi?"

"It's you," Claire confessed.

"Well, of course it is!" agreed Belle.

Claire sighed. "Belle, thank you for being so nice, but the truth is, I'm not a very good painter, either."

Just then, they heard a crash from Maurice's workshop. Belle and Claire rushed over and found him working on an odd contraption.

"Why does your dad invent things?" Claire asked Belle.

"He can't help it," Belle answered. "When he looks at an ordinary object, he sees how it might become something new and different."

The next day was Maurice's birthday, and Belle was going to help Claire bake a cake. Belle practiced with the pastry bag. SQUIRT! The frosting landed all over the baker, but he didn't mind at all.

When the cake was finally done, Belle thanked Claire for her hard work. "My father will love it," she said.

Suddenly, Claire had an idea. "I know how to make this cake extra-special!" she cried.

Quickly, Claire whipped up some more cake batter, frosting, and filling. When she was done, the birthday cake looked just like Maurice's latest invention!

"Claire!" exclaimed Belle. "Don't you see? Baking is where your creativity shines through!"

Claire beamed proudly. She did have a good imagination—and now she knew how best to use it!

The next time Belle went into town, she saw a
crowd gathered in front of the bakery window.
They were admiring a huge cake in the shape of a
castle! The drawbridge was made of peppermint
sticks, and vines of sugar roses climbed up the
castle walls.

Excited, Belle entered the bakery. She saw cookies that looked like teacups, loaves of bread shaped like swans, and cakes that resembled fancy hats.

"Claire, your baking is the talk of the town!" Belle exclaimed.

"And it's all because of you," Claire said, laughing. "Remember when you told me that your father doesn't just see what's in front of him—but what it might become? Well, I realized that I could turn my baked goods into something really special."

"What do you think of Claire's creations?"
Belle asked Claire's father.

"I think they are as sweet and special as my
daughter!" the baker said.